CLEMENCY POGUE: FAIRY KILLER

JT PETTY

SIMON & SCHUSTER BOOKS FOR YOUNG READERS
NEW YORK · LONDON · TORONTO · SYDNEY

CLEMENCY
POGUE

CLEMENCY POGUE: FAIRY KILLER

JT PETTY

SIMON & SCHUSTER BOOKS FOR YOUNG READERS
NEW YORK · LONDON · TORONTO · SYDNEY

SIMON & SCHUSTER BOOKS FOR YOUNG READERS
An imprint of Simon & Schuster Children's Publishing Division
1230 Avenue of the Americas, New York, New York 10020

SIMON & SCHUSTER BOOKS FOR YOUNG READERS is a trademark of Simon & Schuster, Inc.
Book design by Mark Siegel and Jessica Sonkin
The text for this book is set in Cochin.
Library of Congress Cataloging-in-Publication Data
Petty, JT (John T.)
Clemency Pogue / JT Petty.— 1st ed.
p. cm.
Summary: Clever and resourceful Clemency must travel the world to reanimate fairies she has accidentally killed.
ISBN 978-1-4424-3097-6
[1. Fairy tales. 2. Fairies—Fiction. 3. Goblins—Fiction. 4. Characters in literature—Fiction. 5. Humorous stories.] I. Title.
PZ8.P45Cl 2005
[Fic]—dc22
2004001567

FIRST
EDITION

Visit us on the World Wide Web:
http://www.SimonSays.com

FOR LINA & KATE

CLEMENCY
POGUE

PROLOGUE

OF EVERYTHING there is good and bad. This is just how things work.

Ideas, dogs, smells, behavior, songs, guys, machines, cheeses, rabbits, shoes, friends, enemies, days, dreams, fairies; of all of these things and others, there are good and bad.

But rules cannot be viewed except by exceptions, and the exceptions are these: newborn mammals and bees. Newborn mammals are invariably good. Bees, however, are all bad.

If you are a bee sympathizer and find yourself insulted by the above remark, you can petition for the refund of the cost of this book. If this book was a gift and cost you nothing, the author will gladly refund you the love of the giver. If you paid for this book yourself and would like a refund, you may mail the author a self-addressed stamped envelope and a brief note explaining your case.

The author will promptly throw away everything but your address, which will be passed on to the authorities, in the hopes that they will detain you as a bee sympathizer, obviously insane, and in need of either treatment or imprisonment before you can do yourself or others harm.

CHAPTER 1

CLEMENCY POGUE was a child who listened to the stories she was told. It was a quality that saved her life once, and started her on a great adventure.

These stories were spun for Clem by her parents, who were good, kind, and creative people. Unfortunately they worked far away in the mansion of a very rich, very fancy man on the other side of the forest. In the gray of every morning they would march off to work, leaving Clem to her own devices until twilight time, when they would rush back home, her father carrying the evening's meal, her mother percolating with richly embellished stories distilled from the day's events.

"We met a polo player today with a face longer than his horse," she would say, or, "This afternoon the millionaire's nephew was pushed into a river by the lady he was courting. The young man was kidnapped by beavers and ended up as part of a dam. The millionaire is waiting until tomorrow to pull the boy out because the fishing on the other side of the dam is so good."

As Clem's mom unraveled these tales, her father would prepare the meal he had brought home, piling cornucopious gobs of savories and sweets onto the big wooden kitchen table. During dinner Clem would describe what discoveries and imaginations had occupied her day.

"Today," she would say, "I made cold sassafras tea that was sweeter than makes sense. So sweet, so sweet that when I left it alone, it was overwhelmed by its own sweetness. It bubbled and fizzed and could very well change the world."

After supper, from huge earthen mugs, they would drink steaming hot cider or tea or chocolate, and Clem's dad would sift through one of the many old and good stories he knew.

Her dad's stories were far too fantastic and sensible to have taken place in the world we take for granted. He told the old stories like Peter Pan and Wendy. He told stories that he made up as he went along like *The Epic of Gilbert and His Ambulatory Tub*. He told stories that were combinations of the two, mongrel tales like *The Tragi-Comic Blinding of Three Mice*.

The steam from her hot chocolate rising to tickle the cuddle of her chin, Clem sat listening to her dad:

" . . . and as soon as Wendy had spoken, Tinkerbell dropped dead. Dead as a gossamer-winged doorknob.

"'What have I done?' cried Wendy.

"'You've killed her, you brute!' said Peter. His shadow covered its eyes in horror.

"'But how?' she asked.

"'Why, you disbelieved her to death.' Peter explained, 'Fairies are strong, but such delicate things. Not too much more than intentions with wings.'"

Clemency listened, and a good thing, too.

CHAPTER 2

IN EARLY GRAY of the morning, Mr. and Mrs. Pogue marched off through the woods to work.

The sun crept upward sluggishly, fat and golden. As it just passed the horizon, setting aglow the tops of the trees but leaving the forest dark and secret below, Clemency walked out into the woods to begin the day's distractions. There would be no school until the leaves began to turn brown and the days began to shorten. That season was not so very far off, and Clem intended to make the most of her remaining vacation.

She held in her left hand a walking stick that she slung over her shoulder, with a basket hanging from the back end like a hobo's satchel. The basket was for the collection of sassafras roots; she intended to continue with her experiments in fizzing bubbly sweetness.

The walking stick was not for walking. Clem knew that there were places in the forest where danger lurked. And where it did not lurk, danger squatted, crouched, or lounged. There was one place where danger reclined, but Clemency usually avoided it. The walking stick she carried in case of danger, in case she came upon a wolf or a troll who needed to be shown what for.

Clem's pants rasped softly, *swst swst swst,* as her knees brushed with every stride. The pants were made of burlap and were a point of pride for Clemency. She had sewn them herself, and they were quite stylish. Unfortunately, the only fabric she could get her hands on was burlap, so they were a little rough around the seams.

The trees in the forest were as dark as cast iron, older than the dirt they grew in, fatter than walruses, and more twisted than yours truly. A carpet of moss covered the earth and climbed the trees, and was faintly luminous in the green light filtering down through the leaves.

Clem walked slowly about, following her nose toward the patches of sassafras saplings. The tingly, earthy smell led her farther and farther into the deep, dark woods, her path dotted with sassafras that she pulled from the soft earth, shook clean of dirt, and tossed over her shoulder into the basket.

As the sun approached its zenith, Clem

came to a great gorge that dropped abruptly from the edge of the trees. The ground just stopped at a rocky precipice, the exposed roots of ancient oaks dangling precariously into empty space.

Clem, tempter of fate and gravity, kicked a pebble over the edge and watched it tumble slowly down — a tiny white dot that grew tinier as it tumbled through space, falling and falling and falling for ages before tapping against the side of the gorge and bouncing out to tumble farther and farther still, before plunking into the lazy stream at the bottom.

Clem whistled in admiration of the gorge's depth. She felt the weight of her sassafras basket and decided it was about half as heavy as she could bear. She turned and started back home through the woods.

The moss underfoot had dried with the noon sun and crunched slightly as Clem wove her way through the trees. The woods were otherwise quiet. The slight crunch of moss underfoot, the swishing of her burlap pants, and a light rustle whenever Clem shifted her sassafras basket, but no more. Until a small waspish buzz entered Clem's ear for the briefest moment before a burning pinprick presented itself on her basket hand.

"Oh! Drat!" Clem dropped the walking stick and basket, sassafras spilling out aromatically. She looked at her hand, a tiny red dot midway between her thumb and pointer finger, a wasp's sting perhaps. But then another, near her elbow.

"Drat! Drat!" Clem swatted at the air by her elbow and saw the culprit, a tiny insect, slightly smaller than a wasp, the color of yam flesh. The insect descended onto her side and stung her again.

The otherwise peaceable Clem, thrice stung, lost her gentle disposition. She slapped the insect against her side mightily, with a gesture like a very fat man swarthily admiring his own girth.

The insect took no heed, and stung her again, by the navel. She slapped it again, with surely enough force to kill a cow, let alone this bug. Despite the blow, the tiny scoundrel stung her again on the arm.

Clem turned and ran. The insect pursued, diving between Clem's flailing arms and stinging her again several times. Clem stumbled over the giant roots of the ancient trees, calling out a forlorn "Drat!" with every sting.

Clem turned, focusing on the buzzing sound, and swatted at it. She batted the tiny aggressor against one of the great oaks. The tiny monster was stunned momentarily, and Clem turned again, falling over a root, but still moving, still running.

The great trees whirred past like locomotives. In the back of her head Clem could still faintly hear the buzzing. The little beast was on her again. She tried to run faster, but her legs had filled with lead, her lungs were white and frozen for lack of air.

Clem burst through a low hedge of shrubs and out onto the gorge. The exposed roots of the mighty trees dangled before her over the void.

"Oh." Clem was so tired. "Drat." She turned just in time to see the infinitesimal fire bug buzz right up to her face. In the brief instant before it stung her on the tip of the nose, Clem realized what the tiny creature was.

Its body was that of a human, tiny arms and legs, little fingers and toes like threads, a little person perfectly formed save for any bits that you could not show on television. It had a sweet-potato pallor, its skin the vibrant orange of cooked yams. From its back, four dragonfly wings whirred and buzzed like water spattering on a hot griddle.

The tiny aggressor was a fairy, and a mean one. In its hand it held a wand like a tiny cigarette, dull white all the way up with a searing orange tip, which it thrust into the end of Clemency's nose.

Clem swatted at the imp in a mad-ape rage. The fairy dodged backward with malicious grace, dove forward again and stung Clemency's cheek. Only an inch away from her eye, Clem could see the fairy grinning, bubbling over with her own evil.

Clem drew in a great bellowsful of air, shaped her lower lip like the spout of a pitcher, and puffed upward. The fairy was blown from her face, tumbling in midair. Clem raised her arms and brought her hands together in a clap that would easily have brained an elephant.

The fairy emerged from her hands unshaken, grinning like a barracuda. It was invincible. It dove forward at Clem's neck, and she fell backward, trying to evade the tiny burning barb.

She realized an important thing as her legs buckled and she fell backward. She realized that there would be no ground to catch her for the next thousand feet or so; she was falling into the gorge.

Clem's breath left her as the treetops arched away in a rush. Her arms pinwheeled backward. Straight as a board, she fell like a domino into the emptiness.

Hard wood smacked her in the back; the exposed roots of the mighty oaks dangling over the nothing caught and cradled her in their gnarled bark.

Clem was thankful for the roots, not for saving her so much as for delaying her doom. She knew there was no escape. Above her, she could see the whirring wings of the fairy glowing in the afternoon sun. It hovered, seeming to savor the anticipation of cutting off a girl's life after a scant ten years, just on the verge of a great discovery in cold sassafras technology. She knew the fairy would not let her back onto land, and she knew that all that awaited her in the other direction was the "Big Fall," followed by the "Big Splat." She imagined she would not be in any state to care when it came time for the "Big Getting Eaten by Ants." Even if she somehow managed to land in the stream at the gorge's bottom, it would only mean that she would end up soup instead of porridge.

And how could she fight? The fairy was indestructible, as had been amply demonstrated. But then again . . .

Clem, as I said, was a child who listened to the stories she was told. Balanced over her final resting place, and the "awfully big adventure" waiting for her when she fell, the story of Peter Pan and Wendy returned to her.

There was, in the story of the little boy who never grew up, instruction for the extermination of fairies. Clem, secret weapon on her tongue's tip, saw past the certainty of her own death.

She looked at the little yam-colored beast hovering above her and narrowed her eyes like a gunslinger.

"I don't believe in fairies," she said.

The fairy lurched backward and crossed its arms in front of its face. An uncertain, tense moment passed like a fart in a crowd, and then the barracuda grin returned to the fairy's angelic face. The little monster descended on dear Clem.

"I don't believe in fairies!" she said again. "I don't believe in fairies!"

The fairy landed gracefully on Clem's burlap pants and hopped upward toward her face.

"I don't believe in fairies! I don't believe in fairies!" Clem edged backward, trying to keep the fairy away from her face. The roots began to creak, as her weight leaned more heavily on their extremes.

"I don't believe in fairies!" Clem stopped edging and wrapped her fingers tightly around the roots below her. The fairy arrived at her neck, took its burning-hot wand in both hands and raised it above its head like an ax.

"I don't believe in fairies!" Clem shouted, her words tumbling down below her into the gorge.

The fairy's grin faltered. An expression crossed her face as if, despite scale, she had just swallowed a bug. She did a tiny pirouette, and dropped dead as a gossamer-winged doorknob, lying in the tiny hollow where Clem's neck and chest met.

Clem lay for a moment, trying to gather her thoughts, which had scattered like elephants from a mouse. A perilous creaking in the roots below her put an end to her ruminations, and very carefully she turned herself around so that she was facing the edge of the cliff. She gathered herself onto her hands and knees, and the fairy fell from its cradle at the base of her neck.

The tiny imp spiraled down into the gorge, a sunlit glint that flickered and twirled down slowly toward the rocks.

Clem crawled up the fattest root and onto the safety of the ground just as, near the edge of the woods, the ground, in a mighty soil geyser, exploded.

CHAPTER 3

"STOP!STOP!STAHHHHHHP!" a voice bellowed from the shower of dirt.

Clem considered falling backward from the shock, but decided instead to express her surprise with raised eyebrows, as she would not have stopped falling for quite some time.

The geyser of dirt shot up as high as the treetops, and then fell to the ground in sheets, dead leaves fluttering down more slowly. From the earth and chaos purposefully strode, on the squat little legs of a pig, a hobgoblin.

He was three feet tall at best. At worst, he was also three feet tall. His legs and one set of his ears were those of a very fat pig. Each of a second set of ears protruded from either side of his head, ears like those of a hairless rabbit. He had the face of a child, only with the mouth two times too wide, and the eyes three times too large. His great round belly suggested nothing so much as a pumpkin. Left to its own devices, his belly often suggested things like pastries, puppies, doughnuts, dandelions, maidens, or milk shakes. But to the observer,

his belly suggested a pumpkin, for the skin that covered it and the rest of his body was tight and thick like the rind of a winter gourd, the color varying between a slightly yellower pumpkin-orange and the deep green of acorn squashes and alligators. Atop his head sat a tight-fitting metal cap that tapered to a wickedly sharp point.

"Well," said the hobgoblin to Clem, in a voice like apathetic molasses and not at all resembling the great bellow of before. "Now you've catastrophisized every last thing." Then he added, for good measure, "Murderer."

Clem, shocked and discombobulated, was a long time in formulating a response.

"Murderer?" she managed.

"Certainly, you venom-tongued basilisk, you maul-muttering monster. Put seven more notches in your belt, fairy killer." His voice remained overwhelmingly bored.

"But, she was trying to kill me," Clem protested, gesturing to the gorge that held her deceased fairy antagonist.

"Oh, suretainly." The hobgoblin rolled his eyes. "Self-defendo on that account for certain, but what about the other six? If wishes were basketballs and fairies players, you've cleared the court."

"Six others?" Clem said. A glimmer of dawning sorrow appeared in the corner of her eye.

"Seven knives for seven navels and no point wasted on a deaf ear. Seven times you stabbed wicked with what you do and don't believe, and six times you missed before the last hit its mark."

And what the hobgoblin was getting at, slowly crept up on Clem and bit her on the bottom. She had not specified which fairies she did not believe in when she had said, "I don't believe in fairies." Before her misbelief matched her intentions, she had been killing fairies around the world. The phrase was like magic bullets she was releasing into the world that would find a mark, even if not the one she intended.

And certainly, horribly, around the world, the pleasant buzz of winged wishbringers was brought to a stop.

On an icy tundra in the heart of Siberia, the Fairy of Noninvasive Surgery was removing a pea from the ear of a little girl who should have known better. The pea, after the fourth of

Clemency's seven-time proclamation, had company.

In Salt Lake City, Utah, young Jeffrey woke to discover that not only did his tooth remain and he was no richer, but also that a dead fairy lay on the pillow beside him.

In Brazil a fairy prying open a book to teach a boy with love-dimmed wits how to write poetry fell dead and was crushed by words, her tiny fingers sticking out of the pages like twin rooster combs.

Good fairies far outnumber the bad, so the massacre was a mostly horrible thing. But a little good was done.

In jolly old England, for example, a Fire Fairy was playfully relighting the candle on a birthday cake over and over again, denying the birthday wishes of a little girl who had just turned five and was a little blue with her great expulsion of breath. The blue little girl had stopped wishing for a pony with a sidecar, and started wishing only that the candles on her cake would yield to her huffing and puffing. Thanks to Clemency's long-distance disbelief, the fairy was snuffed, and the candles soon to follow.

In Texas the stars shone a little brighter on a herd of cows who were being tormented by the Fairy of Random Prodding. When the fairy fell to the ground and was eaten by a mighty heifer named Sippy, the cows were so happy that they danced a jig. Passersby were convinced it was a miracle, and in many respects it was, for nobody had ever taught those cows anything but samba.

In Hobololi, Mississippi, a fairy fell dead in midair and dropped into the afternoon tea of a horrid little boy. A minute later the boy mistook her for a lemon pip, as that is what she felt like on her way down his gullet.

Around the world death had been scattered to fairies like seeds to pigeons.

"Oh." A tiny sound of infinite sorrow fell from Clemency's barely parted lips.

The hobgoblin had crossed his arms and begun tapping his foot. He looked down the length of his enormous nose at Clem with narrowed eyes that said *For shame, young lady, for shame.*

"I didn't mean . . . ," Clem began. "I was being attacked, and—"

"And you didn't stop to think that maybe

an intricate bureaucracy of make-believe creatures were working full-time to not only stay beyond the edges of human eyes but also maintain a balance between the dark and light, so that the world never grows so over-whelmingly bad as to be evil or so over-whelmingly good as to be boring," said the ugly little messenger. "A balance that was nicely combobulated until your misbelieving banter threw a pixie-grieving spanner into the works and guaranteed twice the work for us survivors."

"I guess not," said Clemency. "I didn't think about that at all." She was at fault completely, helpless. She was quiet for a moment. "Can I fix it?"

"Oh, now she wants to fix it." It seemed like the hobgoblin had his answer ready, and had been simply waiting for the prompt. "Now the murderess wants to wrap a Band-Aid across the globe and leave town before it's time to pull it off, taking all the hair with it."

Quick-witted Clemency, however, realized that there was just such a solution. She had not forgotten the story of Peter Pan. Her voice had been the worldwide poison, perhaps it could be the balm. She clapped her hands and said in a trembling voice:

"I do believe in fairies. I do."

In Texas, a very unhappy fairy was restored to life, and a jigging cow named Sippy became suddenly much, much sadder. After Sippy found temporary relief in the release of a fairy-bearing belch, the whole herd had reason to nix their jig.

"Whoa, there," said the hobgoblin. "Shut your trap before you get caught in it. What about your best and only friend in yonder gorge? What about the Fairy of Frequent and Painful Pointless Antagonism? Every one of your 'believe in fairies I do' is a game of craps that could become a similar exclamation. Seven fairies nixed, now left six, any one of which, their misbeliever risks, from death's reach awoken, by her belief spoken. There's the rub, rube." He motioned with his thumb past Clem, and down to the gorge's bottom where the cruel fairy lay. "Fairies go bad like jarred fruit goes botulistic. Like wrath in death you'll envy after; when that fairy comes back, she'll come hunting for you sure as Sherlock's shrunken shanks. You would be good as dead, and luckier if you were."

"Oh." That little sound of infinite sorrow again. But that sorrow did not last. The thought of the Fairy of Frequent and Painful Pointless Antagonism stoked the fires of Clem's reserve. That fairy had forced her into this, and she would not let herself be whupped by a mean-spirited pixie. It is times like this when all good children come to the aid of themselves, and Clem was good.

"There has to be something I can do to fix it," she said.

"Conceivably," said the hobgoblin dully. "But gobs of notions are conceivable. Clot your imagination with kind wasps and rational adults, but you'll sooner find flying monkeys nestled between your toes. Conceivably—and pay attention—conceivably, if you knew the Fairy of Frequent and Painful Pointless Antagonism's name, then you would gain power over her and you'd be safe. Conceivably."

"If I knew her name?"

"Rumpelstiltskin." The hobgoblin seemed tired, stretched his back. "If a human knows an imaginary creature's name, that human becomes master. That's why we let the humans run the show, mostly. You and your words are big dangerous animals."

Clemency knew the story of Rumpelstiltskin. Here was hope. Clemency narrowed her eyes and rubbed the palms of her clasped hands together in front of her.

"So what's her name?" Clemency asked.

"Nothing worth a life is that easy. We're very secretive about our names. That fairy's never told anybody what to call her; we just know her by her position: Frequent and Painful Pointless Antagonism. That's her job, that's all I need to know. Anyway, my time falls out of my hands like an egg without a shell; you've made me very busy and very late. If you'll just promise me that you won't kill any more fairies, I'll be on my way."

"Where are you going?" Clem was suddenly nervous. She began to pace, the burlap at her knees swishing.

"Java," said the hobgoblin.

"Where's that?" Clem asked.

"Halfway to where we are now, the long way around."

"Sorry?" Clem asked.

"The far side of the globe. But I travel

quick. Straight lines and no potty stops, I could make it there in three beats of a mouse's heart."

"Wow." Clem was honestly impressed.

"So, good day and life and whatever follows. By the by, nice pants."

"Thanks, I made them myself. Though they're burlap," Clem said.

"Good, strong fabric. I have some potato friends who will wear nothing less." The hobgoblin gave a reassuring nod.

"That's true. But they chafe me so."

The hobgoblin's jaw dropped. He stared in wonder at Clem, his fists clenching and spreading like a lung diagram.

"Drad nastit." He shook his head, dumbfounded, defeated. "You wickedly clever child."

CHAPTER 4

"NOW THE WHOLE WORLD might as well know. I'll be a laughingstock. Add some potatoes, I'll be a laughing soup. Reduced to a servant to the whims of every child on this once good earth. Oh, pity, cruel world, poor Chaphesmeeso, he wanted only to save a few fairies. But no. Now, every little bluebird in every big tree, every mole in the ground, every breeze, has overheard this burlap-clad mastermind, and will whisper through the world like an infinitely whistlable, unforgettable song: Chaphesmeeso . . . Chaphesmeeso . . . Chaphesmeeso." Chaphesmeeso sank his large bottom onto the moss. He sighed a deep, deep sigh. He looked up at Clemency. "Killer of fairies, enslaver of hobgoblins. You don't like me much, do you?"

"I . . ." Clemency paused. "I just don't know you very well."

"Well, I don't know if I want to get to know you. You've got a handshake like a lobster." Chaphesmeeso looked down at the ground and shook his head sadly.

"My name's Clemency," she said.

"Ha," said the hobgoblin, not with a whole lot of humor. "Well, self-pity enough." He rocked backward on his great behind and then sprang up onto his feet. "Now that you've got my name, you've got my leash with an option to buy. You wish, I do."

Clemency stopped feeling sorry for the hobgoblin and started planning her solution to all the horrors she had caused. She clasped her hands in front of her and rubbed them together craftily. She narrowed her eyes at Chaphesmeeso.

"How did you know I was killing all those fairies?"

"Everything travels fast underground. Information, too. When you're down in the dirt, you hear things," Chaphesmeeso reported quickly.

"Ah. So you know where all the children are whose lives I've ruined with my fairy slaughter?" she asked.

"Sure, suretainly. There's a little girl in the heart of Russia who was being visited by the Fairy of Noninvasive Surgery. It seems (though even good stories fall apart at the "seems") that this little girl was the victim of a malicious pea. She was innocently supping at her lunch when the lecherous legume fell into her ear. It nestled there and was content to stay, so the girl was visited by our little fairy, who just as she was getting her arms around the pea, was struck dead by Clemency. Ha." Chaphesmeeso lifted his eyes to heaven, satisfied at the last joke, if maybe a little embarrassed.

"Okay." Clemency continued to rub her hands together. "Let's go fix some unhappy children. Line 'em up, I'll knock 'em down. Line 'em up."

"To Russia then?" Chaphesmeeso asked.

"To the heart of it," said Clem.

Chaphesmeeso fastened the chinstrap on his pointed metal hat. "Grab hold of my ears, Clemency."

CHAPTER 5

"NOW LIFT ME UP," he said.

"Won't that hurt?" Clem asked.

"My ears, my dear, have held wild buffaloes at bay. They have tossed the boulder of Sisyphus about like a beach ball. They have tussled with crocodiles, wrestled rabid whales, handcuffed thunder, put lightning in jail." Chaphesmeeso jogged from foot to foot, shadowboxing with his ears. "Lift me up."

Clemency grabbed hold of his rabbitlike ears and pulled him off the ground. Only then did she realize how heavy his metal hat must have been, for he immediately flipped over, the point aimed directly down.

"Ready?" he asked, his upside down mouth a bizarre lemon-wedge shape.

"Ready." Clem had barely pronounced *reh* when the light disappeared in an earthy *fwump* that engulfed her with a great explosion of dirt. There was a sound of great rushing and a *fltftftfltftftftltftftftltfftftft* like a skinny flag in a fat hurricane. She had no sense of direction, but for the feeling of gravity changing around her.

When they had begun, it was pulling her down, headward. Eight seconds into the journey, the gravity was pulling her from every direction. *The center of the earth?* she wondered correctly. After that the gravity grew steadily stronger, pulling at her ankles, but she clutched tightly to Chaphesmeeso's ears, as they plowed upward through the dirt like conjoined supermoles.

Pufwump! A geyser of dirt exploded around Clem as she was pulled upward through the ground on the far side of the world. She landed solidly on snow that packed under her feet. Soil scattered like a tiny rain shower, revealing a glaring white expanse. The last of the black dirt pattered down in white snow, and Clem and Chaphesmeeso were surrounded by the silence of big, fat, softly falling snowflakes.

"That was fantastic," Clem said.

"I do well," said Chaphesmeeso with quiet pride.

"Okay, where's this sad child?" Clem asked.

"There." Chaphesmeeso's finger pointed at a barely visible window that glowed fireplace orange in the dark blue daylight of falling snow. Clem saw it dimly through the fog of her breath.

"Let's go." The girl and hobgoblin trudged through the snow, Clemency's footsteps teardrop-shaped indentations behind her, Chaphesmeeso's a steady trench behind his stubby legs.

The cottage projected a feeling of intense miniature warmth, like a sleeping kitten. Smoke drifted in lazy puffs from the chimney and disappeared into the thick snow. Clemency opened the door a crack and peeked in. The one-room cottage appeared unoccupied, except for a small form, a child, nestled in a quilted bed under the window.

Clem opened the creaking door and stepped softly in, followed quickly by Chaphesmeeso. They crossed the rough wooden floor and stood over the bed.

The child lay sleeping peacefully. Her skin was very pale, her hair short, coarse, and black. Tucked snugly beneath her chin was a great patchwork quilt. The quilt, each square taken from a different worn-out garment donated by family member or friend, was like a map of the many people who had produced and cared for the little girl.

Clemency glanced up and saw that

Chaphesmeeso was smiling sweetly. He noticed Clem's attention and looked away gruffly.

"I was smiling at the pea, not the girl," he said.

"Which ear do you think it is?" Clem asked.

"Peas in ears are all the same to me," said Chaphesmeeso, still embarrassed.

Clem leaned down over the sleeping girl and looked closely at her left ear. It seemed fine. The right ear had a very faint, but angry, pink rim.

"Ah," said Clem.

She leaned her head close to the ear and peered in. It was very dark in there. She could not see the pea or the fairy who was stuck with it.

"Hmm," she said. "I'm not sure what to do."

"No pea charmer, you, hmm?" Chaphesmeeso said.

Clem needed some tools, something to help her see, and some tweezers. She looked around the room. There was a clay stove, and a large wooden table covered with cooking utensils, knives, wooden spoons, tongs. None of it was useful to her. By the front door there were a few coats hung from pegs, and a hat. There was a chair on the other side of the door with a large old woman sitting in it, watching the girl and the hobgoblin with large, hopeful eyes. Next, there was a desk with some scattered papers, pens, an inkwell, and . . . a magnifying glass.

A magnifying glass. Clem walked purposefully over and picked up the glass, when she became conscious of an item lingering in her short-term memory—an old woman with large hopeful eyes.

Clem looked over; the old woman was watching her. She was shaped like a head balanced on top of a heap of grain sacks. She had the appearance of wearing many dresses, and indeed, Clem could see several skirts underneath the outer. Her lips shrank back where teeth should have been, but her teeth had moved out long ago and perhaps retired to a warmer climate. Her eyes twinkled with hope.

"Oh," said Clem. "Hi."

The woman nodded encouragingly and then looked over at Chaphesmeeso. She nodded at her granddaughter, as if to say, *Fix her*. She said something in Russian.

Clem walked over next to Chaphesmeeso, next to the sick child. "Do you speak that language?" she asked.

"I speak human," Chaphesmeeso said.

"What did she say?" Clem asked.

Chaphesmeeso repeated the Russian phrase.

"I mean in my language."

"My job would be so much easier if more humans spoke human," the hobgoblin lamented. "In your little branch of human, she said 'Thank you for coming. I was very frightened.'"

"She knows about hobgoblins," Clemency asked.

"Probably not," said Chaphesmeeso, "but after so many years on the earth a creature gets to expect just about anything."

"Oh." Clem looked over at the grandmother and nodded, as if to say, *I'll do my best.*

The grandmother said something else in Russian.

"She likes your pants," said Chaphesmeeso.

"Thank you," said Clem, smiling smugly. She turned and looked at the child, and lowered herself over the ear, peering into it with the magnifying glass. Nothing. But under the glass, the pink rim of the ear seemed that much more infected, that much angrier. Clem shifted slightly, and there, deep inside the ear, she could see a tiny glint, light reflected off the dead fairy's wing or wand.

She slowly moved her finger toward the ear. As the tip of her finger brushed against the angry pink rim, the child moaned softly in her sleep and turned. Clemency withdrew her finger as if bitten.

"Oh." Clem looked at Chaphesmeeso. "I don't know what to do."

"Not quite the fairy you thought you were?"

"No." She pronounced the word as if she deflated slightly with its saying.

The child, stirred by pain, opened her eyes ever so slightly, and focused on Chaphesmeeso, whose bizarre gourd-skinned face was directly level with hers. Her eyes snapped open, frightened and frozen. Chaphesmeeso grinned evilly and leaned closer to the child. In a harsh whisper, he said:

"Bats and rats
 hide in your hats,
 and bite and carry rabies.
 We hungry trolls,
 we wait in holes,
 and eat up sleeping babies."

He made a scary face. The child drew back quickly.

"Chaphesmeeso! Stop that," Clem hissed, hoping the grandmother had not seen.

"Fine." Chaphesmeeso obeyed.

"How could you?" Clem was miffed.

"I'm not gonna apologize for spoiling the air I breathe or letting a few nightmares out to pasture." Chaphesmeeso shrugged. "I'm a hobgoblin. What do you want?"

"Well, Chaphesmeeso, with the authority of your name I command you not to scare any more children."

"Hey. Whoa. Deny a fish water before you take a child's fear from a hobgoblin. Clip a dove's wings or a human's thumbs. Poop in my breakfast, I won't complain, but don't deny me a child's fear. I'm a hobgoblin, Clem."

Chaphesmeeso seemed honestly hurt. The sick child seemed okay, really. She had gone back to sleep, was even smiling slightly.

"Well." Clem thought a moment. "I guess. I guess you can scare children, just don't scare any of the children who I'm trying to help."

"Done and done. Stick a fork in it, it comes out clean. I won't scare any children you've already scarred." Chaphesmeeso smiled, relieved.

Clem looked again at the sleeping child. Had her ear gotten even redder? She looked over at the grandmother, a wrinkled gray luminary of hope. *Oh, dear,* thought Clem.

Chaphesmeeso looked at her expectantly.

"I'm stumped," said Clem. It was final. It was like a great sinking. She had pushed a child off the edge of a ship, and then thrown the life preserver over the other side.

"Well." Chaphesmeeso looked encouragingly at her. "Every stump is another pile of logs."

"What does that mean?" Clem said.

"I don't know, I was just trying to cheer you up."

"You talk a lot of trash. But thanks." Clem looked at the child. This was hopeless. But if she let herself sink, it meant even more children with their heads below water. *Okay. Keep moving.* She turned to Chaphesmeeso.

"Let's go," she said. *Keep moving.*

"And leave this poor waif with an earful of pixie and pea?"

"Yep. That's exactly what we're gonna do." Clem moved across the room, toward the door. Chaphesmeeso followed.

The grandmother's eyebrows drooped like the eaves of a thatched roof. Her mouth opened and closed, trying to form words. *Come back. Help my child. Don't go.* She only made a small noise in the back of her throat, a sad, hope-flying-away sound, like a kitten dropped from a great height would make on the way down.

Clemency and her hobgoblin walked out into the cold. A little snow blew through the door and settled on the floor.

CHAPTER 6

"OKAY, WHO'S NEXT?" Clemency said. "Line 'em up, I'll knock down the less stable ones."

"Well. In Salt Lake City there's a child just opposite this last one. Something fell *out* of his head. He stuck it under his pillow to exchange it for money, and when the Tooth Fairy arrived, you smote her dead. Young Jeffrey woke to find his tooth had bedded down with the fairy who had come to take it away. He'll have to say bye-bye to that bouncy ball that four bits would have bought."

"Tooth removal." Clem narrowed her eyes. "It's not even attached to his head anymore? I can do tooth removal."

The snow was falling thicker. Clem took one last look at the small, warm, disappointed cabin. *Keep moving*, she thought.

"Let's go," she said.

She lifted the hobgoblin by his ears and braced herself. She was ready for it this time, the changing gravity, the rushing dirt, the explosion of earth, and then the glaring blue overwhelming sky of Utah.

Jeffrey lived in one of a cluster of homes and lawns that looked as if it had dropped from a great height, and spread like an egg on a griddle. The streets were wide and straight and stretched beyond the vanishing point.

"Hard to suss which of these things he lives in," Chaphesmeeso said, rubbing his helmet and squinting at the nearly identical suburban houses.

His tunnel opened in the earth a few feet from a great green mailbox. Large white letters stretching across its side read, JEFFREY'S PARENTS.

"What about that?" Clemency asked, pointing at the mailbox and the house beyond.

"What about what?" Chaphesmeeso asked.

"The mailbox says ,Jeffrey lives here."

"You understand the secret language of mailboxes?" Genuinely impressed, the hobgoblin flopped one of his rabbit ears against the side of the box, listening intently. "I didn't even hear it talking."

"No, no, it's written on the side." Clemency pointed at the letters.

"Ah, scribble talk." He pulled his ear away from the mailbox, grimacing. "I can't read, none of us can. Reading's human magic."

Clemency and Chaphesmeeso walked around the side of the house, wedged open a window, and crawled into the den.

By any hero's standards, their tooth removal adventure was a cakewalk. Girl and hobgoblin were delayed slightly when Chaphesmeeso found a full-length mirror and demanded five minutes to practice scary faces. One of his faces was so well performed that Clem peed a little.

Jeffrey was gone, at school. They found the tooth under his tear-stained pillow, sure enough with the dead fairy lying next to it. Clem was struck by a now familiar pang of guilt.

"All I need is the fairy's name to bring her back to life?" she asked.

"That's all," Chaphesmeeso confirmed.

"But . . . that's easy." A glimmer of hope afflicted young Clem. She looked at the fairy, lying as if merely asleep on the tear-damp linens, and said, "I do believe in the Tooth Fairy, I do."

At those words, with the suddenness of a summer storm, with a flash like inspiration, nothing happened. The Tooth Fairy stayed dead.

"Why didn't that work?" Clemency asked.

"Is your name 'Fairy-Murdering, Hobgoblin-Enslaving, Globetrotting Tailor of Burlap Pants'?" Chaphesmeeso asked.

"No," Clem said, fairly certain.

"Right. It's your job description. Just like 'Tooth Fairy' is her job description." He hooked a gnarled thumb at the fairy's lifeless form.

Clemency nodded. Without the Tooth Fairy's true name, she couldn't return her life. But at least could see that the fairy's work was done.

Jeffrey's tooth was a minuscule little nub, even by baby-tooth standards. Clem picked up the tiny ivory nugget and examined it. A silver-filled cavity dully gleamed in the afternoon light.

"Please, allow me," said Chaphesmeeso, holding out a rough orangutan-like palm.

Clem handed him the tooth, and he threw back his head and popped it down his gullet like a headache remedy. His Adam's apple bobbed cartoonishly as he swallowed.

What do I want? thought Clem, *He's a hobgoblin.*

She patted her burlap pants pockets and found them empty.

"Do you have any change?" she asked the hobgoblin.

"A pile of coins in a hobgoblin's pocket is a mouthful of candy before you can say 'diabetes.'"

"Hmm." Clem looked around. It would be wrong to take Jeffrey's own money to put under his pillow. (Clem had become a staunch moralist after her seventh murder.) She walked out of Jeffrey's and into the living room, and thrust her hands under the cushions of the glaring yellow sofa.

She shortly found three quarters, four dimes, six nickels, one wheat penny, and two normal ones. She returned to Jeffrey's room to find Chaphesmeeso drawing dirty cartoons on a book report that Jeffrey would probably overlook and his teacher probably would not.

Clemency dropped the change onto the linens under Jeffrey's pillow. Chaphesmeeso grinned at her.

"Mine the sofa for change?" he asked. "I'll tell you a secret. The Tooth Fairy does the same thing."

"Who knew?" Clemency picked up the fairy delicately by one foot, holding her between pointer and thumb. The fairy looked peaceful.

She was a lovely little creature with skin the color of vanilla taffy.

"Do we bury her?" Clem asked.

The hobgoblin finished his cartoon with wriggly lines that indicated motion, and hobbled over to where Clemency stood with her victim.

"Again, allow me." He held out a palm.

Clem looked at him for a moment, remembering how he swallowed the tooth.

"Nnnno," she said.

Chaphesmeeso inhaled sharply. "I am shocked," he said in a dull tone. "Horrified and shocked and discombobulated. Does your diseased brain touch your spinal cord? How could you think I would eat so lovely a creature? I'm a hobgoblin. I've got appearances to keep up. A reputation of an appetite for toads and snails, worm heads and guppy tails. Only the uglier puppy dogs. A fairy? Bah." Chaphesmeeso leaned forward meaningfully. "I know of a secret and sacred fairy burial ground that is very close by. If you would be so kind as to allow me, I will see that this fairy's soul will find a resting place at the end of her long, tiring journey." Again he held out his palm, nodded slightly.

Clemency, a little ashamed, gently lay the fairy in his gourd-skinned palm. Chaphesmeeso, in a slow, solemn pace, left the room, leaving Clemency standing over Jeffrey's rumpled bed. She decided to write Jeffrey a note from the Tooth Fairy, explaining the fairy's tardiness.

She found pen and paper and began: *Sorry about being late, but you're not the only kid losing teeth. You see, there was a hockey tournament on the other side of the country, and* . . . She stopped, realized that Jeffrey had probably found the real Tooth Fairy's body, and there was little she could do but hope that a dollar forty-eight would ease and dull his mind. She tossed the note in the trash can.

A great *flush* emanated from down the hall, water rushing out of a big old toilet with a tank like a battle ship. Chaphesmeeso walked back into the room wiping his hands against each other.

"Done and done," he said.

CHAPTER 7

CLEMENCY WAS FEELING BETTER. Despite Chaphesmeeso's growing cruelty, she had solved Jeffrey's problem. She felt she could do this. She could make up for some of the problems she had caused.

"Who's next?"

"Ah," began the hobgoblin in a deep, breathy voice. "Young love. Young love adds color to the cheeks, but that color must come from the brain, which grows decidedly dim. Young love is like ice cream, it's not so healthy but it sure tastes good, and you better lick it up right after it's scooped, or it becomes a sticky, sickly sweet mess. And nobody likes rum raisin young love." Chaphesmeeso nodded knowingly.

"And young lovers are like doves, romanticized and quite lovely, but basically just albino pigeons. They're not so smart. A little American boy vacationing in Brazil met a local girl who took his heart away. Now he's trying to write her a letter to get it back. I guess the missing heart has reduced the blood flow to his brain, because his love letter is the worst thing ever written. A Fairy of Love and Tenderness was trying to open the only book that the boy owns, to show him what good love poetry is like, when she was killed by your misbelief and mashed between the pages."

Clemency thought a moment. Love was not quite her territory, but she supposed she could find her way through it if she had a map. She lifted the hobgoblin by his ears.

CHAPTER 8

THE YOUNG BOY in love sat under a tree atop a mountain that smelled of cloves and sweat. Clemency started up the hill toward him, Chaphesmeeso stayed put at the lip of the tunnel leading to Jeffrey's backyard.

"Come on." Clem nodded her head toward the love-struck fool.

"Mmmmm, no. I know I've said it before, and you must be getting tired by now, but I'm a hobgoblin. Love is brimstone. Sentiment is sulfur. Probably the only thing more frightening than fire."

"You're afraid of fire?" Clemency asked.

"Yeah, a cave troll once mistook me for a marshmallow." Chaphesmeeso rubbed his head and grimaced at the unpleasant memory.

"Did he try to toast you?" Clemency asked.

"No, I was explaining why I'm afraid of love. I'd rather not talk about it. Listen, I'll just wait here, maybe occupy myself by frightening some rabbits or monkeys. You know my name. When you're done, just call it out and I'll have no choice but to come running."

"Oh." Clemency looked at her ugly little companion. He seemed honestly frightened by the proximity of sentiment. She felt a pang of pity pong against the inside of her chest. "Well, I'll see you in a bit, then."

Clemency turned and walked quickly up to the young boy, who jumped when he saw Clem approach, scrambling to cover a sheet of loose-leaf he had been scribbling on with a pencil.

"Whatcha got there?" Clem asked, trying to sound confident and friendly.

"Oh, um, nothing." The boy spoke with an urgency learned by much grade school teasing.

Clem sat down on the ground near him.

"My name's Clemency," she said.

"I'm, uh, Noah," said the boy, and made a weird, silent single chuckle.

He's terrified of girls, realized Clem. *Maybe one bit him when he was younger.*

"How do you do, Noah."

"How do," he said, gritting his teeth slightly.

Looking at the terrified, love-struck boy, probably a year her senior, but shrunk to almost nothing by his anxiety and affection, Clemency realized that this was going to be pretty painful, no matter what. She would get it over as quickly as possible.

"Okay, Noah. I'm gonna be straight with you." She needed a story. "You and whatsername are meant to be. Venus, the goddess of love, sent me here to help you with that poem you're writing. It's a stinker and we both know it. How about you hand it over and we'll talk."

Noah looked at her. His mouth opened slightly, hurt. Maybe calling his poem a "stinker" had not been so hot an idea. Clemency put out her hand and nodded reassuringly.

"Hand it over, Noah."

Noah took a deep breath and gave her the crumpled sheet of paper. Smudges and eraser marks bruised the lined surface as if it had been strafed by fighter planes. Through the wreckage, however, could be discerned a poem:

TO: Becky. FROM: Noah.

Your face is a little gold bell
I hang in the chamber of my heart.
Your face is a little gold bell,
And your tongue is the clapper part.

Your voice makes that little bell tinkle,
Tinkle inside of me.
Now there's tinkle, tinkle, tinkle,
Where my blood is supposed to be!

"Oh." Clem felt that old sinking feeling. "Oh, Noah."

He mistook her words for breathlessness at the poem's beauty.

"Can't you hear it?" he said. "Becky Becky . . . tinkle tinkle . . . Becky Becky . . ."

"Oh, good grief," Clemency said. Where to begin? *Noah, give up. Grow up and hope you fall in love with somebody illiterate. Or, Noah, the world can always use another priest. Or, Noah, love is not for everybody. Maybe you should try data entry.* This was hopeless. She looked again at the poem, as she would have looked at a hamster with a tumor. Hopeless.

"I was thinking" — Noah was gaining some confidence — "I was thinking maybe I should spell 'bell' like the French word for beautiful. Wouldn't that be clever?"

"Oh." Clemency tried to think of something to say. "Your spelling is really right on."

"Well, yeah," said Noah. "I'm a good speller. I like your pants."

"I made them myself." Clemency was like a two-thirds-inflated beach ball that someone had tried to bounce. She sat with her bottom third flattened, feeling weak and hopeless.

Wait: the book. Clemency remembered Chaphesmeeso had said something about a book. Maybe it had some good ideas about poetry in it.

"Do you have any books with you?" Clemency asked.

"Just a Bible," said Noah.

"Good grief," said Clem. *Hooooope Lesssss* sounded in her head like a foghorn. She looked to Noah's right and saw the Bible nestled between the great gnarled roots of the ancient tree. She picked it up.

Between the pages, about a third of the way through, were ten little pale, rose-colored nuggets, like two side-by-side rows of pink mushrooms the size of pin heads.

Horror dawned on Clemency. They were the fingers of the Fairy of Love and Tenderness, sticking out where she was smashed between the pages. She held up the

Bible like it was a sandwich she intended to take a bite out of with her eyes.

There were black specks on the fairy's knuckles. Clemency squinted and brought the book closer to her face. The black specks spread slightly as her eyes focused and, there, a letter written on each finger:

T W I T T.

Next hand: A M O R E.

Twittamore. Clemency thought, *Twittamore?*

She opened the Bible and saw the fairy splayed spread-eagle across the pages, a little flattened, her wings out like a preserved butterfly. The top of the page read, "The Song of Solomon." She read a little bit. It did not even rhyme. *Bang up job, Solomon,* she thought.

Noah leaned forward, to see what she was looking at, and Clemency slammed the book, feeling like she should keep the dead fairy a secret.

Twittamore. It hit her like a flash. (She had never been hit by a flash, but she could assume.) "Twittamore" must be the fairy's name.

She cracked open the book and peered in at the little creature. Noah leaned forward again, and Clemency gave him a firm shove.

"Sit back a second," she said. "I'm trying to help."

She looked at the fairy, which lay across the words: "Thy teeth as a flock of sheep, which come up from the washing." Was this what the fairy was trying for? Good luck, Noah.

She leaned in close to the book and whispered between the pages that cradled the fairy:

"I do believe in Twittamore. I do."

The fairy sat upright like the spring of a mousetrap and struck her head against the page above her. She flinched and covered her head with her hands. She buzzed out of the Bible frantically, bouncing off Clemency's cheek.

Clem reeled, dropping the book, which Noah dove forward to catch. Twittamore rebounded off Clemency's face and came to stability, floating about an arm's length from her reanimator.

She swooped down to hover just outside Clemency's ear canal, and buzzed a sound that Clem could not translate but understood deep in her head, in a voice drenched with subtle sweetness: "Thank you."

The fairy buzzed down to Noah, who was clutching the Bible and staring at the fairy as if into headlights. The fairy paid his shock no attention, but landed gracefully on the crescent of his ear and began to whisper to him.

Noah stared ahead, dazed for a moment, and then frantically took up his crumpled paper and stub of a pencil. He erased manfully for a full forty seconds before flipping the pencil over and scribbling mad affection across the page.

Clemency left them, the young boy in love finally able to express it across the loose-leaf, the fairy whispering maddening sweetness in his ear.

CHAPTER 9

"I HOPE THAT'S done with." Chaphesmeeso was blushing slightly. He scratched at his head through his pointy metal hat.

"All done," said Clemency. "And I brought that fairy back to life." She pulled in her lips until they disappeared and produced a toothless, self-satisfied smile.

"Reanimator, you? No. How did you find her name?" Chaphesmeeso's rabbit ears perked.

"It was written across her knuckles," Clemency said.

"Ah. Clever. Clever, clever." Chaphesmeeso nodded; he approved of this. A grin cracked the gourdish skin covering his face, but then faltered.

He looked down at his own hands as if he had caught them telling his secrets. He looked nervously at Clemency for a moment before splaying his mottled, wrinkled fingers out before her.

"Tell me," he said. "Are any of these marks words?"

Clemency studied the numerous freckles, liver spots, and scars.

"Nope," she said, unable to read anything but a lifetime's worth of digging, "but that birthmark there kind of looks like an elephant holding an ax."

"Egad," Chaphesmeeso said, recovering his composure as he looked down at the pachyder-matological blotch. "Maybe I'll name him Choppy."

"So." Clemency was still riding high on her crest of success with Jeffrey's tooth. "Who's next?"

"Well, now's the time to scratch the rind, Clemcruel or Clemenkind? A fairy in jolly old England dropped dead into the icing of a child's birthday cake. Cream cheese frosting, I believe. The Fairy of Wishes Denied was deny-ing young Amy's birthday wishes by the eter-nal flame of her eighth and final candle. No matter how often or hard Amy puffed, the fairy relit the candle. So, fairy mortar, but fairly moral, I ask: A child's happiness or a fairy's life?" Chaphesmeeso rocked back on his heels.

"A child's happiness. Let's move on." Clemency judged, and well, as a fairy is little more than intentions with wings and a child is possibly everything.

"Fine and good. A fairy's life or the happiness of cows?" Chaphesmeeso asked. Occupied with Clemency, he had not yet heard of the Fairy of Random Prodding's return to life and to the torment of jigging Texan cattle.

"A good fairy or a bad one?"

"Undeniably bad."

"The happiness of cows."

(These last three lines, translated into Japanese, make a beautiful haiku.)

"Fine and good. A fairy's life or the satisfaction of a very bad child?"

"A fairy's life. What's the story?" Clemency was filled to the rim with confidence. Every time she moved, a little dribbled down the side.

"Hobololi, Mississippi. There is a little boy named Sinclair Grimm, an only child, except for a sibling dog. Sinclair's dear old mom loves that dog more than her son, which is frankly understandable. The dog is friendly and smart, and the boy is not. All that we know is that Sinclair is concocting a plan. A plan like a cheap raincoat, horrible and irreversible. A Fairy of Instinct and Wisdom was hovering nearby, to intercede whenever Sinclair started to crank the wheels of his plan, but that fairy dropped dead as a sugar cube into Sinclair's tea, and he drank her. If that boy's actions are any indication of his insides, that fairy's likely grateful that your murderous misbelief drew death's drapes over her eyes before granting her a tomb with a view of his plumbing."

"Hmm. Okay. Let's go to Hobololi, and see what happens." She lifted Chaphesmeeso by his ears, and they were off.

CHAPTER 10

BARRELING THROUGH THE EARTH like a tunneling locomotive, Clemency heard huge hollow *clangs* like stones being thrown against a tin shed.

Clang. Clang. Clangclang CLANG.

"Drad nastit." Chaphesmeeso muttered a moment before they burst up through the earth in Mississippi.

CHAPTER 11

CHAPHESMEESO HAD DARK stones stuck to his pointy metal hat. They clung squat and heavy like toads.

"Drad nastit," he said again, and clustered his grubby fingers around them. He pulled mightily and the stones came loose one by one. "Stickystones," he said.

The stickystones dropped to the ground, clustered together, and stuck fast.

"Wow," Clemency said. She picked up a few of the stones and they snapped together in the palm of her hand. She pulled them apart and they snapped together once more. She pressed them against her head, and they fell away, back into her palm.

"They only stick to one another," she said.

"And my hat." Chaphesmeeso groaned. "And the tips of my poor little toes."

Clemency looked down. A little dark rock was stuck to one of the horseshoelike rings nailed under Chaphesmeeso's hoof.

"Huh," Clem said, figuring. "They stick to metal. I suppose."

"Well, suppose all you want—it's free." The hobgoblin threw the last of the stones onto the ground.

Clem held a stone about two inches from Chaphesmeeso's hat. It pulled in her hand like a small bird. She released it and it jumped to Chaphesmeeso's hat with a great *clang*.

"Hey, stop that, you wicked tormentuous imp. I've had kindlier mosquitoes buzz in my ear."

Chaphesmeeso moodily pulled the magnet from his hat and dropped it to the ground. "Oughtn't we go help this child?"

"Right," Clem said. She hiked up her pants and set her jaw. "Show me the way."

"Ah," said the hobgoblin, and placed one tough finger against the side of his nose. He sniffed meaningfully. "The perfumed earl," he said.

Clemency's brow lowered. She sniffed the air. She could indeed smell perfume. She sniffed again. "The earl?" she asked.

"Earl Grey," Chaphesmeeso explained, and stomped gracefully back into a drape of kudzu. Clemency followed, and they trekked through foliage so intensely green that Clem feared it would rub off on her. Chaphesmeeso's thick green-to-orange skin almost seemed to disappear in the vegetation. The air was thick and slightly sweet, and in the distance, through the woods, clouds moved along the ground like the misplaced ghosts of rogue elephants.

Through the wilderness they trudged and then through a sudden thinning to a huge, ordered garden of the same plants. The girl and the hobgoblin stayed on the edge of the wilderness and watched a very thin and very pale boy sitting cross-legged in front of a great mound of broken china teapots and cups.

The boy had five teapots lined up in front of him, and a tower of unused cups and saucers that would not have stood out in Pisa. The boy took a draining last slurp from a teacup and tossed it over his shoulder as if he had spilled salt and wanted to catch the devil off guard. The cup shattered against the pile, adding its fragments to the mass. He picked up another cup from the stack by the tree, poured tea into it, squeezed lemon into the tea, and then began to drink it with intense determination.

"He seems a little more than thirsty," said Clem.

"A little more than thirsty, a little moron surely." Chaphesmeeso grumbled. "His name is Sinclair, and he is a very bitter boy. He owns a dog named Chester, who is clever and kind and, despite his limited vocabulary, a charming conversationalist. Sinclair is none of these, and even less of other things. The only thing he has discovered he is good at so far in life is bleeding from the nose, which he does copiously, often, and with fervor. Sinclair's mother has noticed the qualities lacking in her son and present in her dog, and has dished out her love accordingly. Sinclair is a bitter little pip. And he is plotting something overwhelmingly wicked—we just don't know what."

"That's real sad." Clemency looked with pity on the boy, who seemed to be drowning his sorrow and lapels in Earl Grey. "I hope he doesn't hurt the dog."

Another teacup smashed against the pile behind Sinclair.

"He must be about to burst," Clemency said. "Let's go introduce ourselves to the dog, see if we can figure this out."

"Right. Dogward ho." Chaphesmeeso led them around the perimeter of the garden and to a huge, pillared, white house. It was roughly the size of a breadbox, only much, much larger. Clem and Chaphesmeeso squeezed in through an opening in a screen of the porch, and wandered into the house. They followed the hobgoblin's nose into the kitchen, where a great mangy mutt lay on the tiles, soaking up the cool.

Chester, the dog, looked shocked at Chaphesmeeso for a moment, and then at Clemency, and then grinned wide, breathing happily.

"Hello, sir," said Chaphesmeeso.

"Hey, pup," said Clem, and squatted down next to the dog. She scratched his back and he lifted his ears, as if to say, *Scratch behind these*. Clemency did, and Chester showed such pleasure and gratitude that Clemency was overwhelmed with warmth and satisfaction.

Chester made a charming little grumble and rolled over to show heaven his belly. Clemency scratched it briefly and then patted him twice. Chester flipped over onto his feet and licked Clemency's cheek once, quickly, with a dry tongue.

As Clemency stood, Chester waddled over

to Chaphesmeeso. He sat down casually before the hobgoblin and offered his paw. Chaphesmeeso took the paw and shook it formally.

"How do you do?" said Chaphesmeeso.

Chester glanced briefly at Clemency and then back at Chaphesmeeso and gave him a wink that said, *Oh, not too bad, you know how it goes: humans. But such is our lot.*

Chaphesmeeso laughed politely, and Chester made another charming little grumble.

"Do we have to worry about anybody else in the house?" asked Clem, looking around.

"No, not a-tall. Maybe a few servants here and there, but servants and imaginary creatures have an understanding."

Clemency scratched Chester's head again. "This is a good dog."

"A noble mutt." Chaphesmeeso smiled in agreement at the pooch.

A door slammed from the back of the house, and hurried childish footsteps stomped across a wooden floor.

"Sinclair," said Clemency. She and the hobgoblin walked on tiptoes, following the sounds of stomping feet. Through a hallway, a den, a great living room, and then they could see him, standing pale and malicious through a doorway.

He was standing in the middle of a room that was all dark wood and expensive furniture. He cast a slow, sweeping gaze across the room, arcing like a lighthouse of bitterness on the rocky shores of filial ingratitude. The room was some kind of a study; it reeked of authority and tradition. His gaze fixed on an object out of sight, against a far wall. He stood gazing at it for a moment like a matador, and then charged out of sight.

Clemency and Chaphesmeeso eased forward to the doorway and peeked through. Sinclair was standing next to a beautiful antique sofa, all cushioning and wood, shined by years of loving use. A lever extended from one of its ends, and Sinclair's angry little fingers wrapped around it like a gang of worms.

With a crazed, baboon look in his eye, he pulled the lever sharply. There was a great *sproing,* and the sofa unfolded and shot forward into a bed.

"Hah!" snorted Sinclair in anticipated triumph.

He yanked the lever the other way and with a dangerous *gniorps*, the bed sucked itself back into the form of a sofa, springs coiling and creaking noisily.

"Ahhh." Sinclair sneered like Napoleon Bonaparte, only scarier. He gave the lever another mighty yank and the bed shot out and slammed down onto the floor again. Sinclair leaped onto the bed and began jumping up and down.

Clemency could hear the tea sloshing around inside of him.

The soft tumbling patter of four-footed steps clumpered up behind the girl and the hobgoblin, and Chester walked up and sat between them, watching the bitter, bouncing boy. The dog tilted his head to the side, confused and concerned.

Sinclair gave one last mighty bounce that bent a spring inside the bed, and then fell to his knees. He grabbed a cushion from the sofa bed and brought it to his mouth. He opened his chompers impossibly wide and tore into the cushion, like the cotton-starved caboose of a vengeful porcupine.

The girl, the hobgoblin, and the dog were

flabbergasted. Sinclair ripped out huge chunks of fluff and cotton, and tossed them about with his head. He whipped back and forth, tearing at the cushion, trailing streamers of cotton that clung to Sinclair like baby opossums. Fluff wrapped itself around Sinclair's head, stuck to his clothes. When the cushion was mauled and torn beyond repair, Sinclair spitefully dropped it to the ground with another horrible laugh. He grabbed another cushion, the tea still sloshing within him, and brought it to his toothed pit of destruction.

Chester's eyes were wide as saucers (the flying kind) and his jaw dangled. He was making a small whimpering sound.

Chaphesmeeso watched the boy with slight disgust, but admired the craftsmanship. Clemency was aghast. In fact, she was two ghasts. Her mind began to form around Sinclair's sinister plot.

She looked down at Chester, and then at Sinclair, who had finished with his second cushion and was on his hands and knees, tearing at the bed itself. He was acting like a bad dog. The boy was acting like a bad dog.

"He's framing Chester. His mother's going

to think that the dog did this," she said.

Chaphesmeeso and Chester looked at her.

"The ghoul," Chaphesmeeso said. "A boy is a dog's best fiend, indeed." He patted the dog with sympathy. Chester looked from girl to hobgoblin, and then back at the boy, hopeless.

Sinclair stood up and tore into a third cushion, still raving like a berserker. And then the true horror began.

It was an image that would burn itself into Clemency's retina like the burning of the *Hindenburg.*

Sorrow and disgust.

The terrifying unthinkable potential of the human spirit.

An action so despicable, so pointless and cruel, that every person the witness meets for the rest of his life is doubted, simply for sharing species with the transgressor.

Sinclair paused, sloshing. He still held the cushion between his teeth, but his hands left it, traveling south, as if for a holiday. They were not on holiday, though; they had a purpose. A dark, effluvial purpose.

The hands settled on his pants.

"No," said Clemency. Chaphesmeeso covered

his eyes. A weak whimper escaped Chester and flitted away.

There was an unzipping. A pause. A sound like eggs frying on the hot stones of Hades, as Sinclair tinkled on the bed.

Tinkled like a horse back from a long night of drinking with its friends.

Tinkled like a punctured water tower.

Tinkled like a bell suspended in the heart of a young lover.

Maybe you should stop reading, and take a little time to think about how bad this is.

CHAPTER 12

CLEMENCY COULD NOT just stand by and let this happen. Maybe the Fairy of Instinct and Wisdom would have done something by now, for it was certainly too late to stop it.

Pee-damp fluff lay scattered about like the dead and dying on a battlefield. If only Sinclair's mother would walk in the room now, everything would be so clear. She could see that the dog was innocent. She would understand that Sinclair needed more attention, more love. Clemency wished she could freeze the moment, could seal it in amber and wait for Sinclair's mom to arrive.

It was the time for action. Chaphesmeeso still covered his eyes; his rabbit's ears thrust themselves into the pig's ears to block out the sound. Chester was on the verge of hyperventilating. Clemency took a deep breath.

She clenched her fists at her sides and strode into the room. Sinclair looked up and saw her. His eyes widened and his face flushed apple red. Clemency paid him no mind, but strode across the room to the edge of the sofa bed and wrapped her hand around the lever. She looked Sinclair in the eye.

"Be brave. This is for the best," she said, and pulled the lever.

Gniorps! With fluff strewn all over his head and chest, the cushion locked between his teeth, and peeing still, Sinclair buckled and fell into the bed as it sucked itself into a sofa.

Clemency stumbled away, shaken with the horror that she could still see silhouetted against the black of her eyelids every time she blinked. Chaphesmeeso slowly took his hands from his eyes.

"Thank you," he said.

Clemency nodded at the hobgoblin. The sofa had a large boy-shaped lump in it, and a small puddle developing underneath.

"When his mother gets home, she'll understand," Clemency said. She turned to Chester, who was leaning against Chaphesmeeso's leg, catching his breath.

"Chester," she said, "when Sinclair's mom gets home, I want you to lead her to him. Try to make her understand that he just needs more attention."

Chester nodded, and then pushed himself

upright. He padded over to Clemency and sat before her and offered his paw. Clemency took it and shook it.

"You're welcome," she said.

CHAPTER 13

"Okay, who's left?"

"Well," said Chaphesmeeso. "Nobody. Except the girl with a pea and a fairy keeping her brain company."

"Ah." This pained Clemency slightly. "Well, I guess we better go back." Perhaps she had gained some experience in her quest that would grant her newfound wisdom.

She looked around at Hobololi. Crickets were beginning to sing in the lush woods. Sinclair's house stood behind them like a monument.

"Okay then," said Clemency, "back to Russia." She lifted Chaphesmeeso by the ears.

CHAPTER 14

SIBERIA WAS DARK and white. The shower of
dirt from Chaphesmeeso's tunnel finished pat-
tering to the ground, and an eerie snow-muffled
silence settled in the air.

The white expanse stretched out perfectly
smooth to the trees, drifts in great mounds rising like giants hiding under their sheets. The
snow glowed, reflecting the light from the clear
nighttime sky, the moon oddly absent, and
every individual of the millions of stars a dis-
tinct pinprick through the darkness.

Clemency rubbed a little soil out of her eye
and looked at the small cottage they had visited
earlier. The snow had covered their tracks to
and fro, the home squatted glowing and warm
against a blank white canvas.

Chaphesmeeso pulled a few small stickystones from his hat and dropped them to disappear beneath the snow. He grinned and took
a deep breath, enjoying the cold night air. He
smacked his hands against his taught gourdish
belly.

Clemency sighed, the fog of her breath

momentarily covering her view of the cottage.

"Let's try again," she said with a heavy exhale, unsure of herself. She trudged toward the cottage, her progress heavy and slow through the shin-deep snow.

She knocked on the door as she eased it open and stepped into the warmth. The grandmother had been tending to the fireplace, and stood at the knock.

She made a slight noise in the back of her throat, somehow indicating that she had hoped for the return of the girl and her hobgoblin. The grandmother drew in her lips with a worried expression, nodded welcome, and gestured toward the bed.

From the doorway Clemency could see that the child had gotten worse. The third of her head around her ear was the angry pink color. Clemency knew that kind of discomfort, the way you imagined the sore spot like a rotten bit on a tomato, the way you could feel your pulse in it.

Wet footsteps on the wooden floor traced from the door to the child's bedside, following Clem and Chaphesmeeso.

The grandmother returned to her seat by

the door. She had complete faith in her visitors' healing powers.

Clemency bent close and looked in the ear. A little more wing showed, as if the child's head was making slow progress at pushing its guests out. If only she could see the fairy's hands, she could reanimate her. The Fairy of Noninvasive Surgery could solve this in a moment, she was sure.

Clemency stood straight and looked at Chaphesmeeso. She caught him looking down at the child with concern, and he was briefly embarrassed. There was nothing to say between them. Clemency could not help this child and they both knew it.

Clemency looked at the grandmother, and then down at her shoes. The last of the snow had melted off the cuffs of her burlap pants, leaving small wet marks on the floor.

The foghorn again sounded in her head: *Hovoope Lesssssssssss.*

She looked at Chaphesmeeso.

"The fairy could solve this, couldn't she? She could do it easy," she said.

"Suretainly. If she wasn't so busy decomposing."

Clemency had grown accustomed to his sarcasm and let it pass.

Clemency thought for a while. "If I brought the Fairy of Frequent and Painful Pointless Antagonism back to life by mistake, would she be able to find me all the way over here in Siberia?"

"Oh, yeah. She has the same brand of netherknowledge as myself. She would probably be here in about two minutes."

"Oh, dear." Clemency examined her shoes again. And then the metal of Chaphesmeeso's shoes. A thought struck her. "What are fairy wands made of?" she asked.

"Same junk as my hat," said Chaphesmeeso.

"Hmm." Clemency began to form a determination. "Well then. I'm gonna bring this fairy back to life the same way I killed it. Here's mud in your eye."

She cleared her throat and rubbed her hands together in nervous anticipation. She took a deep breath and clapped her hands: "I do believe in fairies. I do."

Underneath Utah, a very confused Tooth Fairy woke up floating in everything else Salt Lake City deemed flushable and thought, *How am I going to get this off my wings?*

Clemency clapped her hands again, "I do believe in fairies, I do."

In jolly old England, a Fire Fairy found that a certain child who had wanted a pony with a sidecar for her birthday had been given, instead, a frog. To the frog, a living fairy looked much more appetizing than a dead one.

"I do believe in fairies. I do."

A certain fairy would need all of his instincts and wisdom to get out of Sinclair's lower intestine. He managed it disguised as a tapeworm and was immediately instrumental in Sinclair's life. It was the Fairy of Instinct and Wisdom who led Sinclair's mother to her son, trapped in the sofa he had chewed and peed upon, for Chester, the dog, was inclined to leave him in there.

Clemency took another deep breath. "I do believe in fairies. I do."

At the bottom of a deep rocky gorge, far below moss-covered trees older than the dirt they grew in, a tiny hand emerged from a bubbling creek and pulled a very angry fairy onto a rock. She shook the water from her wings. *Vengeance, vengeance,* she thought as she jumped into the air, her wings buzzing her toward Siberia.

"Do the math, Clemency, your nemesis fairy is on her way," said Chaphesmeeso in a hush. Clemency looked at him a moment and her breath faltered. But she would not be deterred, "I do believe in fairies. I do."

The child twitched with an itch deep inside her head. The fairy stumbled out of her ear, tumbling in midair until her wings found equilibrium. She shook her tiny head, wiped a slight residue off her wand and flicked it with disgust onto the bed.

The grandmother was smiling; this was the kind of magic she expected.

The Fairy of Noninvasive Surgery gave Clem one curt professional nod. It was a neutral gesture, balanced between *I detest being killed* and *Thank you for giving me life.*

The fairy turned her attention back to the ear and plunged down into it.

Chaphesmeeso leaned in for a better look, and Clemency did the same. They could see nothing but the darkness of ear.

The child drew in a sharp breath, exhaled it in a whimper, and then fell silent as the snow.

She barely drew in any air at all for several seconds; her eyes tightened shut.

Chaphesmeeso squinted and leaned in closer. The dark hole of the child's ear was impenetrable.

Then a glimmer. And the fairy fluttered out backward, her head and arms still in the hole. She planted her feet on the rim of skin-covered cartilage on either side and pulled mightily.

She heaved upward, and Clem and Chaphesmeeso could see she had stuck the wand into the pea and was pulling on it like a handle. They could see the green-gray mass of the pea, straining against the sides of the child's ear.

Polp! The sound was small and utterly insignificant as the pea crossed some fleshy threshold and popped effortlessly out of the child's ear. The pea hopped off the fairy's wand, carried by the momentum of her pulling, and flew in an arc over the child's head, bouncing once on the mattress and falling to the floor.

I will not invite you to examine the last thing you ate by going into a detailed description of how the pea looked, but you can trust that a day and a night in a child's ear does nothing for a legume's appearance.

Chaphesmeeso strode forward and stomped on the pea, squishing it utterly.

"That little pea won't be hurting anybody else," he said.

The grandmother was standing, and clasping her hands before her, a grateful grin stretching over her face. Clemency and Chaphesmeeso stepped to the side, so that she could see her grandchild.

The grandmother strode across the room and sat gently on the edge of the bed and hugged the child without lifting her. She said something softly in Russian, over and again.

Chaphesmeeso leaned toward Clemency. "You have maybe a minute and a half before your nemesis arrives."

CHAPTER 15

CLEMENCY'S FIRST THOUGHT was to get far away from the child and her grandmother. She had caused them enough pain already. She walked quickly to the desk from which she had earlier retrieved the magnifying glass, and after brief rummaging, found it. She stuck the magnifying glass into one of the ample back pockets she had sewn on her pants, and crossed to the door, Chaphesmeeso on her heels.

The Fairy of Noninvasive Surgery was waiting by the front door, and she flurried out into the cold night as soon as Clemency opened it. The fairy disappeared skyward among the stars.

Clemency stepped out from under the eaves of the cottage and scanned the horizon. Chaphesmeeso shut the door behind him, the warmth vanishing like fogged breath, and stepped out next to Clemency.

Clemency turned to the hobgoblin. "I need a stickystone. A big one."

"That'll take a little time," Chaphesmeeso said. "We're talking other hemisphere."

"Fine," said Clemency, and began trudging out into the snow, away from the cottage. Chaphesmeeso followed. "How long will it take?"

"Four minutes if I'm lucky. Which means four minutes." The hobgoblin scratched at a leathery cheek.

"Get to it." Clemency continued through the snow, her breath trailing out behind her like steam from a locomotive.

"Suretainly." Chaphesmeeso stopped and watched Clem trudge off for a moment. "Burlap pants *and* brave. A good kid."

The hobgoblin nimbly bent at the waist until the point of his metal hat had pierced the snow and was touching the frozen earth below. Clemency glanced once briefly over her shoulder, and saw Chaphesmeeso kick his legs into the air. His hands became a digging blur, and he dropped into the earth as if swallowed.

Clemency turned forward, her eyes set on the expanse of snow before her. Far in the distance she could see a line of pine trees, no more than a barbed black shape against the horizon.

She looked back at the cottage; it was not so far off as she had hoped. Her progress through the snow was much slower than her usual spry pace. She leaned into her walking, hopping a little with each step to lessen the pull of the snow.

She continued on until her lungs ached from the cold, dry air, and her eyes were blurry and tired. She stopped, panting, and looked back at the cottage. She was far enough. Hopefully the fairy would attack only her.

Clemency stood in the middle of the snowy expanse and caught her breath, tried to calm herself. The stars above seemed even brighter than before—they stretched in glowing ribbons across a sky that graded deepest blue to an empty black.

She scanned the horizon again. She saw movement in the orange square of the cottage window, and a moment later a rectangle of the same light widened from a line next to it. The door was opening, and the grandmother's silhouette stepped into the rectangle of light.

The old woman followed with her eyes the trail Clem had left in the snow out to where she stood alone. The grandmother squinted, and with some effort, focused on the little girl standing in the cold.

The grandmother disappeared back into the cottage for a moment, then reappeared, now burdened with a great quilt that she held bunched in front of her. She started out toward Clemency, walking in her footprints.

Clemency watched the old lady approaching through the cold night. Clem could picture the old woman being stung to death, little freckles of pain dotted across her kindly face.

"Stop! Go back!" Clem shouted. Though her voice carried like crystal over the snowy silence, she was speaking in a tongue that did not fit the old woman's ear. Clem shook her head dramatically, waved her arms, and motioned back toward the cottage.

The grandmother stopped, still within a stone's throw of her home, and watched. Clemency repeated her gesture, slowly, more elaborately. The old woman took a cautious step forward, and Clem shook her head in wide arcs. The grandmother stopped, took a step back. Clem nodded and made a grateful shooing motion. Confused, the old woman cocked her head. She was listening to something.

Clemency held her breath and tried to listen. Very faintly, so soft it could be mistook for imagined, there was a buzz. In the snow-induced silence so definite that it almost made your ears ache, she could hear the buzz of the approaching fairy.

"Oh. Oh, no." Clemency shooed more drastically at the grandmother, but the old woman was listening intently to the buzzing.

The buzz was growing louder and louder. A faint whir to it, an angry sound like hornets make and bumble bees do not.

And then Clem could see it. A red star fell from the sky. The tiny red dot of the fairy's wand was floating against the black strip of distant pines.

The grandmother could see it too. She watched it race directly toward the girl who had helped her grandchild. The old woman turned and ran back into her cottage.

Clem did not notice, her eyes fixed on the approaching red dot. She raised her hands uncertainly. She knew running would not work. She hoped she could fend off the fairy until Chaphesmeeso got back with the sticky-stone.

The red dot still looked far away, when all of a sudden the fairy seemed to materialize

right next to her, lit by the searing incandescent tip of her wand.

Clemency let out a brief cry and swatted. The fairy rode the air currents that swept around the blow, effortlessly evading it, and then swooped forward and stung Clemency on the collarbone.

Clemency jumped back and swung again, this time with two hands that converged on the fairy. She caught it between her palms with a great smack, and then another.

The fairy was annoyed. It lunged at Clem again, and Clem swung and missed. She stumbled back in the snow that was starting to work its way under the cuffs of her pants, and swatted again. She contacted with a downward blow that knocked the fairy out of the air.

The fairy fell into the snow, the water crystals sizzling and evaporating against her wand.

Where are you, hobgoblin? Clemency thought, taking rapid steps backward to gain a little more space and ready herself for the fairy's next attack. She was shivering fiercely, the twin paint shakers of cold and fear clamped on her heart.

Clemency saw a line in the snow tracing an

arc around her. The line collapsed a moment before she felt a sting against her right shoulder blade. The fairy had tunneled through the snow and come up behind her.

"Drat!" Clemency spun, and the fairy spun with her, another sting to the back, and another.

Clemency threw herself onto her back in the snow and rolled over, scrambling to her knees. She looked down just as the fairy got to its feet. She pounded at the nasty imp with a balled fist.

The fairy flitted into the air at an angle, and Clemency's fist struck the cold hard ground. The fairy stung her forearm and lunged at her neck.

Clemency dodged and rolled, stood and ran. She turned and swatted wildly, missing the fairy, but rotating her body enough that its searing wand missed its mark, hitting a button on her shirt.

Clemency looked desperately about, searching for Chaphesmeeso. The horizon was empty, a sting at her elbow.

"Drat!" Frustration and pain and anger. Clemency stumbled forward, running through the snow. She could not fight the fairy with her hands. It had not worked before and it would not work now. The snow dragged at her feet like a nightmare. Her only hope was the hobgoblin. It was not so great a hope.

A sting burned the small of her back, another marked her calf. She tried to swat at it as she ran, and saw the tiny aggressor for a moment before her. The fairy's wand cast a red glow in Clemency's fogged breath. The fairy was grinning again like a barracuda.

The hobgoblin was nowhere to be seen. Clemency could not have run much farther, and was not even given the chance. The ground dropped below her, a dip in the earth covered by a drift in the snow.

Her knees buckled as her feet plunged down, and Clemency fell face forward in the dark white nonglow of cold, nighttime snow.

She rolled onto her back, her face so cold that she no longer shuddered. So cold that the snow was not melting from it. The fairy hovered just beyond her reach, looking down on her with scorn and an utter lack of pity. The red tip of her wand glowed searing against the distant stars.

CHAPTER 16

CLEMENCY THOUGHT how strange it was that she was not cold, and was grateful that she would not die in a chill. Her legs, under her trusty burlap pants, were in fact still quite toasty.

Bless these pants, she thought.

The fairy hovered over Clem like a nose over savory pie, anticipating the moment before indulgence. But she had savored enough. Her wicked smile stretched back in anger, and the tip of her wand glowed hotter still, past red to the weird orange of an electric range. Past orange to a dull pink that seemed almost to dip into white. The fairy drew back for the charge.

And then a sound like the war cry of Hollywood Indians carried across the snowy plain. A cry John Wayne could have let forth, leading the cavalry, if John Wayne had been an old Russian woman.

The fairy jerked back and looked over her shoulder. Clem raised her head off the ground uncomfortably and looked toward the sound.

The grandmother charged through the snow toward the evil little fairy, a broom raised over her head like a samurai's sword. She charged in great wobbling steps, moving in unstoppable lumbering strides, each one threatening to tip her over like a drunken cow.

Valkyries only wish they could make a sound like she made. It would have frightened banshees.

The fairy turned to face her new adversary, but barely had time to raise her wand before the grandmother took a final leap, swinging as she landed in a toadlike squat. As her mighty feet thundered into the frozen earth, the straw of the broom snatched the fairy from the air and drove her into the snow. The old woman raised the broom and struck it into the snow again and again, as if trying to beat out a fire.

Clemency struggled up into a sitting position, snow falling off her in clumps. She got to her feet, watching the old woman rage with the broom against the tiny evil imp. She seemed to be working out all of the anger and frustration from seventy years in a cold part of a mostly unfair world.

The broom came down with a final swat

and rested in the patch of snow it had flattened. The grandmother panted, smiling slightly, and looked at Clem. She said something in Russian.

"Thanks," Clem said.

A shooting star fell through the sky above; Clemency jumped as if she were going to be attacked. She realized what happened and sighed, almost chuckled.

The grandmother cautiously raised the edge of the broom, looking for the corpse of the fairy. She raised it more and more, and then removed it altogether—the beaten snow was empty. She looked at the broom; it, too, was empty.

"Hmh?" she said, in the nonsurprise of the elderly.

She slung the broom over her shoulder and held a hand out to Clem, an outstretched hand that said, *Come, I will make hot chocolate.*

Clemency got to her feet and took a step toward the old woman. She smelled smoke. The faint, acrid smell of smoke from straw. Clemency paused. Rising against the starry night, a faint line of smoke rose from the business end of the broom.

Clemency pointed.

The grandmother turned her head, and just as her eyes converged on the thin line of gray rising into the black, the broom combusted. It burst into a great ball of flame that roared like a starved bear.

The fairy, hiding among the husks, had waited with her wand touched to a fiber until it caught flame.

The grandmother shrieked, and raised the broom and struck it against the ground, hoping to beat out the flames. The flames flared out against the beaten snow with a great *whoosh*, and a tiny, angry speck emerged from the tongues of fire.

The fairy swooped upward and hovered an inch from Clemency's nose. With crossed eyes, Clem could just barely see the terrible little creature nod toward the grandmother, wrinkle its nose, and wink. The fairy was saying, *Watch what I do to the old lady, because you're next.*

Clemency swung at the fairy. It easily dodged her hand and flitted toward the grand-mother. A whale's length away, the earth exploded in a cookies-and-cream geyser of dirt and snow.

The old woman shrieked again and hopped

backward, dropping the broom. The broom brushed against Clem's pants and she side-stepped frantically, brushing the flames from her cuff.

Chaphesmeeso walked out of the falling shower of earth and snow, something dark in his hand, about the size of a scoop of ice cream.

"Well done, hobgoblin!" cried out Clem.

The grandmother shrieked a third time and began to hop from foot to foot, slapping at her behind. *A Russian victory dance?* thought Clem, and then realized that the old woman was being stung by the fairy.

Clem stepped forward to try to help her, but the old woman knocked her down as she bounded toward the burning broom. She fished it from the snow, the straw end still ablaze, and swiveled with the broom out-stretched, swinging at the vile little dot hover-ing in the air.

Clemency had to flatten herself against the snow not to be struck by the burning cleaning implement. She could feel the heat as it passed within inches of her head. Clemency scrambled backward like a crab, getting out of broom range.

"Give me the stone!" she shouted at the hobgoblin.

Chaphesmeeso was frozen where he stood, staring in horror at the old woman with her burning broom. He pointed a trembling finger.

"Fire," he said softly. "Fire."

"The stickystone, Chaphe, quick!" Clem called out.

"Fire." Chaphesmeeso's eyebrows huddled at the top of his head in fear, like bashful caterpillars kissing. His rabbit's ears drooped.

The old woman shrieked again and slapped her collarbone. She took off across the snowy field at a gallop, swinging the broom blindly behind her as she went, shrieking every five or six steps at another sting.

"The stickystone, drad nastit!" Clemency called out. "Now, Chaphesmeeso!"

The hobgoblin was watching the flames race across the snow, the old woman and her aggressor lit by a flickering orb of orange light.

"Chaphesmeeso, throw me the stone!" At a direct command, the hobgoblin's gaze flicked over to the girl. He nodded once, drew back his arm, and threw her the magnet. It struck the ground well out of Clem's ability to catch it.

"Bang up job, hobgoblin," Clemency muttered.

But the hobgoblin did not hear her. He dropped to the ground, burrowing into the snow to get away from the distant flames.

Clemency ran to where the stone had disappeared into the shin-deep snow.

The old woman yelled in frustration and pain. Clemency could see that she had fled a third of the way to the cottage and dropped the broom, swatting at her body in a fury as the fairy attacked her again and again. Clem could see the tiny red dot swoop and sting, pull back and pause; swoop and sting, pull back and pause; over and again. The old woman stumbled toward her home, shrieking and swatting, the broom's flickering orange light casting her shadow for miles over the flat, white plain.

The grandmother did not realize what she was doing. But Clemency, from her vantage, could see that she was leading the wicked fairy back into her home. Once it had finished with the old woman, leaving her polka-dotted with pain, the fairy would turn its attention to the little girl.

Clemency did not intend to let that happen.

She searched frantically for the stickystone, came up only with a handful of snow. In frustration she formed it into a ball and threw it at the tiny dot antagonizing the grandmother.

Hardships reveal a person's talents. Clemency threw snowballs like Spaniards lick stamps: with deadly accuracy.

The snowball caught the fairy in a pause, imbibing her in its mass and carrying her to the ground. Clemency let out a whoop of satisfaction and leaped into the air.

The fairy struggled out of the snow and shook it from her wings. She rose into the air and saw the source of the snowball.

Clemency fell back to the ground, feeling about for the stickystone. She fumbled blindly, finding only the dirt below and stray twigs dried and frozen by winter.

The fairy ignored the panting old woman cowering over her, and buzzed toward the girl who had killed her in the first place. All the old vengeance and rage came back.

Clemency looked up and saw the fairy on its way. She rose, forming another snowball, and let it fly. The fairy was ready and feigned right, the snowball only brushing her leg, spinning the fairy in the air. Clem let fly another immediately, and it struck the fairy while she was disoriented, knocking her back, but not to the ground.

The fairy's rage grew, pushing the tip of her wand to white hot and past it, the intense non-color glare of a light bulb. She began again toward Clemency, more slowly, more angrily.

Clemency felt about in the snow: no stickystone. She gathered another snowball and launched it. It flew straight and true at the fairy, sure as a comet. The fairy stopped in midair and waited; at the precise moment she thrashed about with her metal wand in a blurred intricate pattern of sizzling heat.

The snowball turned from snow to water to mist instantaneously. The white ball just disappeared into steam with a fizzle, the moisture collecting on the fairy's face and wings and freezing into tiny glimmering crystals.

Clemency felt around her. Nothing there, like the stickystone had melted into the earth. The fairy was advancing. Clemency stood and threw another snowball, missing completely.

She threw another and the fairy did not even stop, but vaporized it with her wand in midflight. Two more snowballs met similar fates. Clemency had only moments before the fairy was on her.

She dropped to her hands and knees, intent now on the stickystone, knowing snowballs would do her no good. The ground was empty, tauntingly void of magnet. She spun, searching a wider swath of snow, frantically feeling about. She could hear the buzz of the angry fairy approaching, could almost hear the hiss of the tip of its searing hot wand as it cut the night air.

And then her foot struck something heavy and round, about the size of a cat's head. Clemency spun and pulled the stone from the ground. It was dark and too heavy and almost perfectly round. Clemency picked it up, stumbling to her feet, pulling a fistful of snow with the magnet.

The fairy was almost on her. Clemency balled the snow around the stickystone, packed it tight, and pulled back her arm. Her eyes narrowed on the white-hot dot of the wand, she tensed the muscles in her arm, and catapulted it forward.

The fairy grinned at the futility of the little girl's gesture. She reared back and executed the whirring parry with her wand. The snow vaporized instantaneously, revealing the magnet underneath, which pulled the wand to it like a frog retracting its fly-laden tongue. The fairy, pulled by her wand, smacked against the round rock, and was held tight while it fell to the snowy ground.

Clemency leaped again in triumph and ran to where the stone had dug a trench in the snow with its landing. She could hear the fairy buzzing angrily, saw the glow of its wand coming from the trench.

Clemency stooped down over it and picked up the stickystone. The fairy was attached, pulling angrily at its wand, stuck to the stone like the stem of an apple, her wings a furious buzz.

Clemency brought the stone close to her face and whipped the magnifying glass from her back pocket. The fairy buzzed and raged, inches from Clemency's face. She could feel the intense heat of its wand through the stone and in the air around the tiny creature. Clem slid the lens between her eye and the fairy and focused on the tiny creature's knuckles. There she could see, spelled out across the digits:

T I N K A S I N G E

Clemency's eyes widened. She dropped the glass into the snow and held the stickystone out before her. She drew in a breath and:

"I don't believe in Tinkasinge," she said, barely more than a whisper.

Tinkasinge let go of her wand and shot back in the air, staring fiercely at Clem. She crossed her arms in front of her face as if she could block her coming demise, but it was useless. She did a tiny pirouette in the air, croaked, and fell dead as a gossamer-winged doorknob into the snow.

CHAPTER 17

THE GRANDMOTHER TOOK Clemency and Chaphesmeeso into the cottage and made them hot chocolate. She dried Clemency's clothes in front of the fire and introduced them to her granddaughter.

They thanked one another, promised to visit, and thanked one another again.

Clemency yawned mightily. It had been a long day.

Clemency and Chaphesmeeso said their good-byes. Chaphesmeeso apologized to the child for having frightened her earlier, said he was a hobgoblin and could not help it. The grandmother gave Clemency an unexpected hug, which was a pleasant thing.

The grandmother and her grandchild waved from the door as Clemency and Chaphesmeeso trudged out into the snow.

"Take me home," said Clem.

CHAPTER 18

CHAPHESMEESO'S TUNNEL opened in the forest just outside of the property surrounding Clemency's home. Here night was only beginning to fall. The sun was well below the horizon, and the sky glowed salmon pink.

"Well," said Clemency, "I suppose that's it, then."

"For now," said the hobgoblin, sounding bored as ever. "Of course, you know, so long as you've got me by my moniker, I'm yours to play like a cheap harmonicker."

"Excuse me?"

"Is my name 'Evening Clothes'?" Chaphesmeeso asked.

"No," Clemency said.

"Then you can't wear it out. Just call me and I'll pop up; I don't have a choice in the matter. Though I might show up even if I did. Have a choice, that is."

They stood for a moment among the huge ancient trees, uncomfortable, unsure of what to say.

"Oh, I saved something for you." Chaphesmeeso pulled a round stickystone from his hat, the one Clemency had used to down Tinkasinge. "A little something to tie a forget-me-knot around. A souvenir of that time you killed Tinkasinge. Or that other time you killed Tinkasinge."

"Thanks." Clemency took the rock. "I think these stickystones could be an important scientific discovery. I'm trying to think of what to call them. It's like they've got a magic net that grabs metal—"

"No, no, no," said Chaphesmeeso. "The sticky stone's just wrapping, scrap it. Look closer."

Clemency did. And there, stuck to the dark, dull surface, was a tiny sliver of gleaming silver. Tinkasinge's wand.

"The wand!"

"Suretainly. That's a powerful splinter, a direct translation between intention and fact."

"You mean magic?" Clemency stared. "Could I make magic with this?"

The hobgoblin touched his nose and winked. "In dreams. Only imaginary creatures have intentions distilled enough to prove the imaginary real. So only as the imagined you in your own imagination can you imagine the imaginary true. Overstand?"

"I don't even understand," said Clemency.

"Put the wand under your pillow tonight before you sleep. Whatever you dream will wake up with you."

Clemency's eyes widened, her mouth dropped slightly.

"I? . . . My dreams will come true?" Clemency asked.

Chaphesmeeso nodded.

"What if I have a nightmare?"

"You're tough; you can handle it. Anyway, I ought to be off. Nobody likes a hobgoblin when he's on." Chaphesmeeso wiped the palms of his hands together. "That was good work today, Clemency."

He turned so his back was to Clemency, and leaned forward until the tip of his pointy hat touched the soft moss of the forest floor. He looked up at Clem from between his legs.

He said, "Luck." And then he dropped into the earth in a blur of motion.

"Thank you, Chaphesmeeso," said Clemency.

Swish, swish, swish. Her burlap pantlegs rubbed against each other as she walked back to her home.

That night Clemency began her story during dinner. It lasted through dessert and well after hot chocolate. Her parents listened, and applauded when it was over.

Snuggled warmly in bed at the tale's end, Clemency thought how nice it was to be home.

EPILOGUE

THE DEAD FAIRY'S WAND lay beneath her pillow.

Clemency dreamed of a fat, happy little bumblebee that buzzed from flower to flower like Saint Nick on Christmas Eve. The insides of the flowers were soft and glowed in the mid-day sun. Pollen stuck to her fuzzy legs in great sweet yellow clumps. She could taste honey, and realized that it was not from having eaten a spoonful, it was simply the taste of her mouth.

Down the road, whenever Clemency would

think of this dream, she would hear a faint *pop*, and find herself looking through the sectioned black eyes of a fat, happy bumblebee. She wobbled slowly around through the air, from flower to flower, collecting pollen and tasting honey. She was a good bee.

So I suppose that nothing is invariably bad. I hate to admit it, but there is always a potential for good in the world. I was wrong. Bee sympathizers will get a full refund.

The End

Printed in the United States
By Bookmasters